Hello! I'm the Doctor, and this is my book. Only it isn't like other books, because I'm going to tell you what happens at the end first – I escape! From space prison! Amazing, eh? But while I was locked up I kept a diary, and you can read some of it in the pages that follow – along with loads of top-secret intelligence reports from my friends (and even some enemies). Enjoy!

CONTENTS

THE DOCTOR'S PRISON DIARY

Direct from my psychic paper!

JUDOON MAXIMUM SECURITY FACILITY CRIMINAL RECORD

▶ **PRISONER**
The Doctor

▶ **ORIGIN**
Gallifrey (disputed)

▶ **CRIME**
Classified

▶ **SENTENCE**
Whole-life imprisonment

▶ **DANGER RATING**

1 2 3 4 5

DAY 6,935

Morning! Or is it afternoon? Could be evening. Time's all relative!
Usually I'd tell you all about how I'm a wanderer in time and space – travelling the galaxies, fighting monsters, righting wrongs and generally having an amazing time. But I haven't been doing much of that lately; not since I got arrested by the Judoon and thrown in space jail. So, here's the current situation . . .

I'm the Doctor, prisoner of the Judoon and currently serving a life sentence in a tiny cell on a barren rock in deep space. I've been separated from my ship, the TARDIS. And, even worse, I've lost my fam – Yaz, Ryan and Graham. They're my gang, my crew, my three right arms. Three right arms – that would be pretty cool, actually! Maybe next time I regenerate . . .

Oh yeah, I can regenerate too! When my body gets old, or knackered, or blown up, or blasted with radiation, a bright orange energy starts fizzing out of every cell and I change into someone completely different. Usually that's a bonus, but it's going to make my whole-life sentence feel really, really, really, really long.

NO! GO!

As you can see from my tasteful wall art, I've been here a while, so I thought I'd start a diary to keep my mind occupied. I don't have any pens or paper, but I do have a single brain cell that's always tethered to my psychic paper, keeping track of everything for me and showing you the pages. Clever, eh?

Would you like a tour of my cell? Over there is a wall. Behind me is another wall. Then, to my left and right, two more walls. Food gets beamed in, empty plates get beamed out – no opportunity to jab the guard with a spork. In fact, there are no guards, just bossy holograms. I have a few neighbours – I'll introduce you to them as we go along. No sticking your hand through the bars though, or you might never see it again.

Being in here has given me time to think. I recently found out I'm not the person I thought I was, which is confusing – even when you've been as many different people as I have. I don't have all the answers yet, but as soon as help comes I'll be out of here and off to find them! Fancy joining me for the ride?

FIENDISH FOURS

Can you spot four matching monsters in a row? They could be across, down or diagonal. There are eight sets of four to be found – get hunting!

Kerblam! Men
Deadly delivery robots.

Cybermasters
Cybermen made from the bodies of Time Lords.

Thijarians
Ancient, time-travelling assassins.

Pting
Very cute, but very dangerous.

Dregs
Mutated humans from Orphan 55, a potential future Earth.

Skithra
Nasty alien scavengers.

Ribbons
Troublesome creature of the Antizone.

Stenza
Ruthless trophy hunters.

ANSWERS ON PAGE 61

DALEKS!

THE ARCHIVE OF ISLOS

PART 1

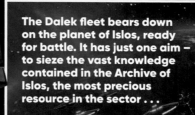

The Dalek fleet bears down on the planet of Islos, ready for battle. It has just one aim — to sieze the vast knowledge contained in the Archive of Islos, the most precious resource in the sector . . .

INHABITANTS OF THE PLANET ISLOS. THE *DALEKS* ARE COMING. YOU WILL *SURRENDER!*

THE SHIPS ATTACK!

FTOOM!
FTOOM!

A DALEK EXECUTIONER FLIES IN AND TAKES AIM.

EXTERMINATE! EXTERMINATE! EXTERMINATE!

BZZZT!

AAAAAAAARGH!

ORBITAL WEAPONS PLATFORMS ARE DESTROYED. THE PLANET IS *DEFENCELESS.*

THE DALEK ASSAULT CONTINUES, BUT THE ARCHIVE REMAINS UNSCATHED . . .

INSIDE, THE ROBOTS WHO RUN THE ARCHIVE CALCULATE THE DAMAGE TO THE CITY.

WE SERVE THE ARCHIVE. IT MUST BE PROTECTED. WE MUST HOLD THE DALEKS OFF.

FTOOM!
FTOOM!
FTOOM!
FTOOM!

ATTENTION! ATTENTION! I WILL SPEAK TO THE ARCHIVE OF ISLOS.

I AM THE *CHIEF ARCHIVIAN* OF ISLOS. HAVE YOU COME TO APPLY FOR A *MEMBERSHIP CARD?*

THIS IS THE DALEK EMPEROR...

YOU ARE DEFENCELESS. YOUR MASTERS HAVE ABANDONED YOU . . .

YOU WILL SURRENDER THE ARCHIVE TO ME!

CONTINUED ON PAGE 21

9

MONSTER CELLMATES

THE WEEPING ANGEL

» PRISONER
Angela

» ORIGIN
Unknown

» CRIME
Theft of
potential energy

» SENTENCE
Held in quantum chains

**» DANGER
RATING**

1 2 3 4 5

WINGED
GREY
STATUE

FACE
SWITCHES
FROM ANGELIC
TO FERAL IN
ATTACK MODE

PHYSICAL
FORM DECAYS
WITHOUT
ENERGY

»» Weeping Angels
turn to stone
when observed
thanks to their
quantum-lock defence.

»» They're very fast,
but only when no other
creature is looking
(even another Angel).

»» To avoid making
eye contact with
their fellow
Angels, they
cover their
eyes with their
hands, which
makes them look
like they're weeping.

»» Anything that holds
the image of an Angel,
like a reflection or a TV
screen, can become
an Angel!

KNOWN SIGHTINGS:

**1938, 2012
New York, Earth**

**2007
Wester Drumlins, London, Earth**

**FIFTY-FIRST CENTURY:
The Wreck of the *Byzantium*,
Alfava Metraxis**

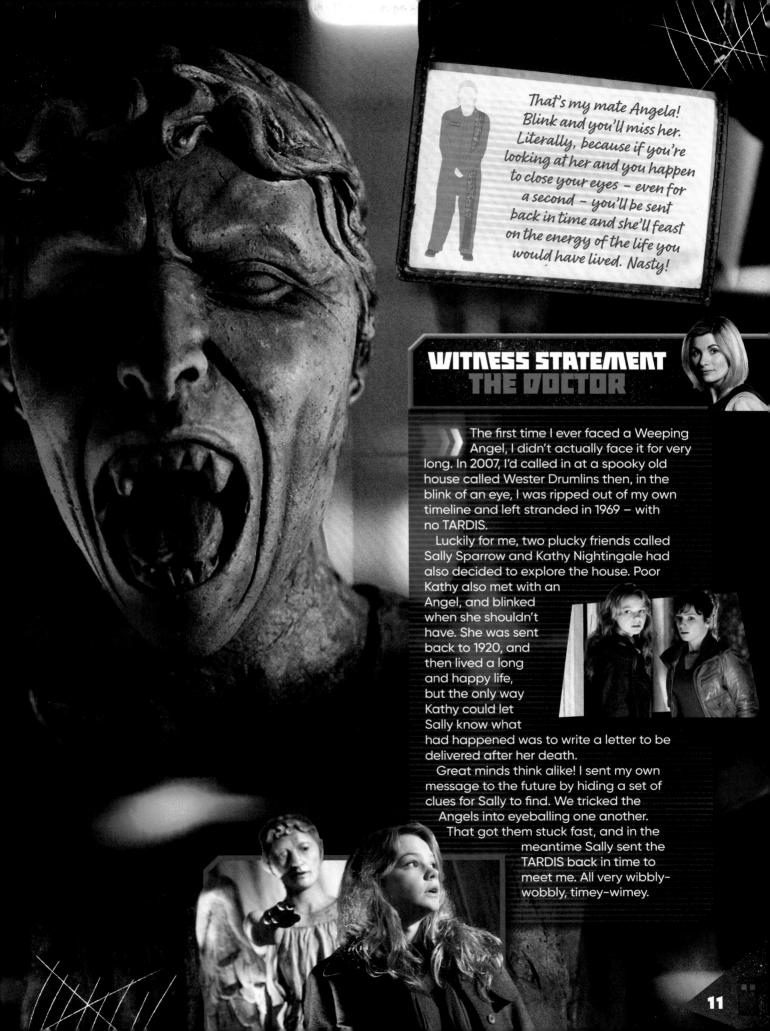

That's my mate Angela! Blink and you'll miss her. Literally, because if you're looking at her and you happen to close your eyes – even for a second – you'll be sent back in time and she'll feast on the energy of the life you would have lived. Nasty!

WITNESS STATEMENT
THE DOCTOR

The first time I ever faced a Weeping Angel, I didn't actually face it for very long. In 2007, I'd called in at a spooky old house called Wester Drumlins then, in the blink of an eye, I was ripped out of my own timeline and left stranded in 1969 – with no TARDIS.

Luckily for me, two plucky friends called Sally Sparrow and Kathy Nightingale had also decided to explore the house. Poor Kathy also met with an Angel, and blinked when she shouldn't have. She was sent back to 1920, and then lived a long and happy life, but the only way Kathy could let Sally know what had happened was to write a letter to be delivered after her death.

Great minds think alike! I sent my own message to the future by hiding a set of clues for Sally to find. We tricked the Angels into eyeballing one another. That got them stuck fast, and in the meantime Sally sent the TARDIS back in time to meet me. All very wibbly-wobbly, timey-wimey.

All About YAZ

FULL NAME
Yasmin Khan

ADDRESS
Flat 34, Park Hill estate, Sheffield

JOB
Junior police officer, Hallamshire Police

I was happy as a junior police officer – my dream job! Then the Doctor came along, and everything changed.
   Suddenly I was doing all the same stuff, but my beat was the entire universe! Now I get to use all my old skills along with some new ones that aren't in the police manual. It's everything I wanted from life (times a thousand!), and I never want it to end . . .

MY HOME

I know it says up there that my address is on the Park Hill estate, but the place I feel most at home is inside this magical blue box. It belongs to the Doctor and it's called the TARDIS – Time and Relative Dimension in Space. Why is it so special? Well, it can travel anywhere, any time – past, present or future. Oh, and it's also bigger on the inside.

MY FAMILY

I love this bunch – even if they drive me crazy sometimes . . .

This is my mum, **Najia**. She's a super-efficient hotel manager who can organise the day-to-day stuff, but also deal with giant-spider infestations or toxic waste. Mum is always pleased when I make new friends too, cos that's not always been easy for me.

Here's my dad, **Hakim**. He's a big fan of conspiracy theories, no matter how many times I tell him there's a rational explanation for most things. Well, as rational as anything involving the Doctor can be! He'll always make you welcome. Just don't try his pakora – it's rank!

And this is my little sis, **Sonya**. She still lives with Mum and Dad and has had more career changes than I've met alien species, but her heart's in the right place. She can be annoying, but she's always there for me. I even miss her a bit when I'm off travelling with the Doctor, but don't you dare tell her I said so.

MY FRIENDS

OK, I say they're my friends, but these guys are more like family too . . .

This is **the Doctor** – and there's nobody quite like her. Brave, bold, funny, scary and everything in between. When she's around, life is amazing. But occasionally she vanishes for months on end, and that hurts so much that I sometimes wish I'd never met her.

Aww, **Graham** and **Ryan**. The greatest grandad-and-grandson combo in the galaxy. We had the adventure of a lifetime together. They've gone off to do their own things back in Sheffield, but we'll always have each other's backs. Fam forever!

And **Captain Jack Harkness** is one of a kind. Probably just as well. Imagine two of him! Together! At the same time! The universe just couldn't deal. Underneath the attention-seeking and wisecracks, there's a wise old soul.

MY CAREER

My police training can come in handy at unexpected times . . .

EMERGENCY RESPONSE
When a UFO crashed in the Peaks, who was the first-response officer? **PC Yasmin Khan**, of course! I secured the scene, took witness statements and met a very important new friend for the first time.

SURVEILLANCE
Krasko was an alien who tried to mess with **Rosa Parks'** timeline so she wouldn't become a legend of the civil rights movement. I tracked Rosa's activities to make sure we could get her to the right place at the right time – the bus where she famously refused to give up her seat, and the rest is history

UNDERCOVER OPERATIONS
I posed as a Kerblam! warehouse worker to get intel on the shady stuff happening there. While undercover, I used my interview skills to gather information and my restraint training to stop a suspect from escaping.

CAPTAIN JACK'S DALEK FILES

EVOLUTION OF THE DALEKS

I'm Captain Jack Harkness, and over the centuries I've learned a thing or two about the Daleks. I've even been killed by them a couple of times – long story.

It always pays to know your enemy, which is why I'm sharing my secret files – so you can be ready the next time the Daleks invade. Because they will *always* come back . . .

THE BEGINNING

The Daleks come from the planet Skaro. Nice place, if you like desolate wastelands and hands growing out of the soil. Before the Daleks became the Daleks, they were the Kaleds, who looked pretty much like you and I do (although maybe not quite as handsome as me). The Kaleds were in a thousand-year war with Skaro's other inhabitants, the Thals, and everything and everyone started to mutate from the nuclear and chemical pollution it caused.

DAVROS

The Kaleds' chief scientist, Davros, came up with a plan to make sure his side would survive. It was one of the most monstrous schemes in history – to turn them into Daleks!

Davros used a motorised chair to get around. Look familiar? He took his own support system to the next level, creating an armoured travel machine that would sustain every life function.

MUTANTS

Mutation can be a slow process, but Davros didn't want to wait. He sped up evolution to grow pure Dalek mutants to fill his travel machines. Unfortunately for Davros, his new creations thought they were purer than he was and exterminated him.

14

SHELL SHOCKS!
Dalek shells are made from a tough bonded polycarbide armour called Dalekanium. Other materials can be used in an emergency, including glass and Sheffield steel.

DEFENCE SHIELD
A Dalek shell has a force field that can stop most forms of attack. Energy weapons bounce right back, and bullets fade to nothing!

COLOUR CODING
A Dalek's rank is often shown by its colour. Generally, standard drones are bronze and high-ranking Daleks are red or black.

SENSE GLOBES
The bumpy parts on the lower half of a Dalek shell are sensors that contain the unit's self-destruct mechanism — and hide rocket launchers!

THE TIMELESS CHILD

I used to think I knew all my faces – even one that I tried to keep secret. But thanks to the Master, I now think there's a whole lot more to my past than I'd ever imagined! Here's everything I know so far . . .

Thirteen. That's my official designation in the long line of Doctors. Now you might think it's unlucky to be the Thirteenth Doctor, but that's a load of rubbish. By the time I got to be Thirteen, I'd been Grumpy, Silly, Daring, Bonkers, Dashing, Clashing, Baffling, Charming, Brooding, Victorious, Magical and Scots – the Seven Dwarves have nothing on me! But I was the lucky one, because I had the best bits of all of them, and the best of me too.

1
2
3
4
5
6
7
8
WAR
9
10
11
12
FUGITIVE

But what if I wasn't Thirteen? What if there were more of me? Impossible, right? Maybe not. My oldest enemy, the Master, turned up and dragged me to the ruins of our home planet, Gallifrey. 'Everything is about to change,' he told me.

He led me to the Chamber of the Matrix, where all Time Lord knowledge was stored. It was the one thing he'd spared when he destroyed Gallifrey, so he could tell me its darkest secret.

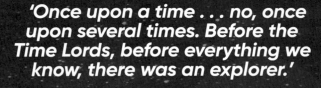

'Once upon a time . . . no, once upon several times. Before the Time Lords, before everything we know, there was an explorer.'

He told me of a Shobogan woman called Tecteun. One of Gallifrey's native people, Tecteun yearned to travel and explore the stars. So off she went. On her travels, she found the Boundary – a gateway to another dimension. And she found a child there, abandoned and alone.

Tecteun adopted the child. On Gallifrey, the child had an accident and died, but while Tecteun mourned something incredible happened. A bright orange energy started fizzing out of every cell in the child's body, and she changed into someone completely different. Now, where have you heard that before?

Tecteun was desperate to understand the child's special powers. And when she learned the secret of regeneration, she stole that knowledge, splicing the ability into her own genes.

And that's how the Time Lords came into being. The Timeless Child founded our entire society.

Oh, and did I forget to mention? That child is me.

But I don't remember any of this – the life I thought I'd lived wasn't my first. How many lives have I had? I reckon there's more of this story to come . . .

MONSTER CELLMATES

THE OOD

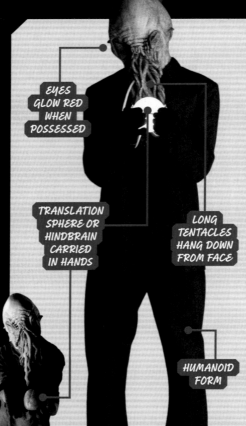

JUDOON MAXIMUM SECURITY FACILITY CRIMINAL RECORD

》 PRISONER
Bonnie

》 ORIGIN
The Ood-Sphere

》 CRIME
Violent disorder

》 SENTENCE
Solitary confinement in restraints

》 DANGER RATING

EYES GLOW RED WHEN POSSESSED

TRANSLATION SPHERE OR HINDBRAIN CARRIED IN HANDS

LONG TENTACLES HANG DOWN FROM FACE

HUMANOID FORM

》 Ood don't speak – they're a herd species and communicate telepathically.

》 They're naturally peaceful creatures, but they can become violent if their telepathic ability is abused.

》 The Ood are born with two brains: a forebrain in their head, handling basic functions, and a hindbrain carried in their hands, to deal with emotions.

》 Enslaved Ood have their hindbrains removed and replaced with translators, which convert their thoughts to speech so humans can understand them. They're also weapons.

》 They're great singers.

KNOWN SIGHTINGS:

2015

4126

4221

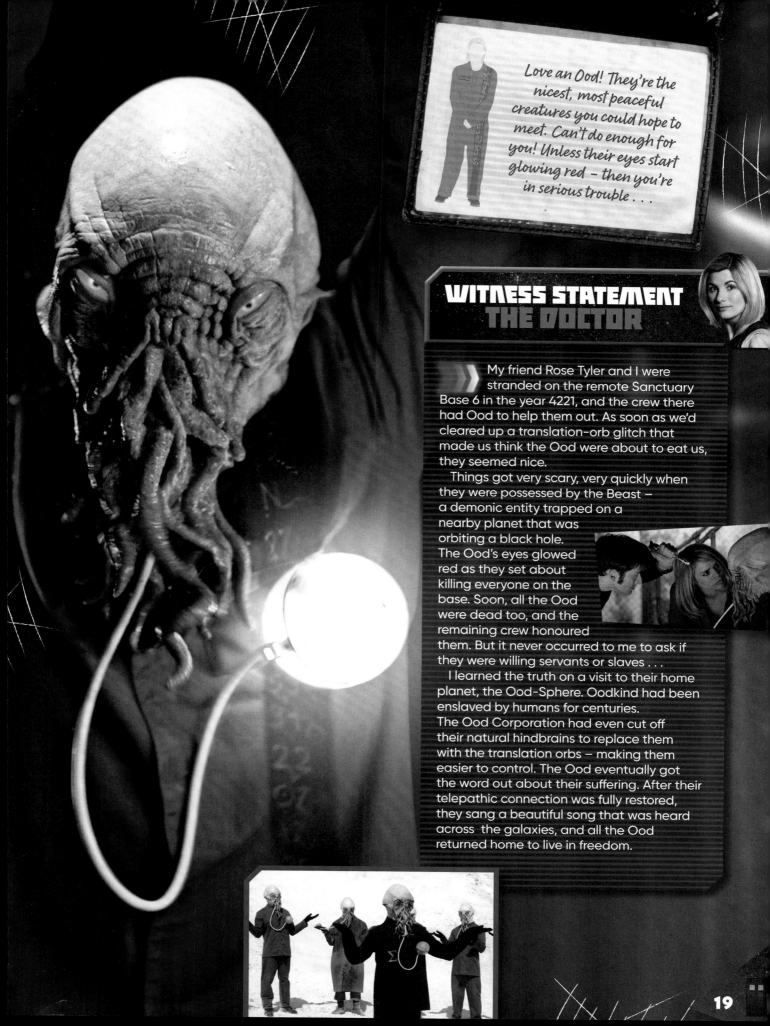

WITNESS STATEMENT
THE DOCTOR

My friend Rose Tyler and I were stranded on the remote Sanctuary Base 6 in the year 4221, and the crew there had Ood to help them out. As soon as we'd cleared up a translation-orb glitch that made us think the Ood were about to eat us, they seemed nice.

Things got very scary, very quickly when they were possessed by the Beast – a demonic entity trapped on a nearby planet that was orbiting a black hole. The Ood's eyes glowed red as they set about killing everyone on the base. Soon, all the Ood were dead too, and the remaining crew honoured them. But it never occurred to me to ask if they were willing servants or slaves . . .

I learned the truth on a visit to their home planet, the Ood-Sphere. Oodkind had been enslaved by humans for centuries. The Ood Corporation had even cut off their natural hindbrains to replace them with the translation orbs – making them easier to control. The Ood eventually got the word out about their suffering. After their telepathic connection was fully restored, they sang a beautiful song that was heard across the galaxies, and all the Ood returned home to live in freedom.

19

BEAT THE JUDOON

CATEGORY: Judoon language.
TASK: Identify fifteen words in grid.
PUNISHMENT FOR FAILURE: Imprisonment

```
D J P J L G W U Z H E R Y V D H V T H Q
H X P K X S R H D N C O U D U F V Z A U
D H I U I X N N P I I W Y M S I C Q Y C
P F I R K I H P F Q D V Z Y L Z A D K V
U Z N T X F S G N M N X A X S B I Y X Z
O W P V Q N Z Z C Q U O Z X S J F N C U
I C M P M G L Q P Z C V Q I C G T L G L
J U H D S P Y V E D H Z N N M P W C W N
H T E B F P B L W D E R D I T I O Y V G
E K U N Q C X W I X X S G B K M U V I M
Q W C R K R O X M O I Z I F D B S F O C
U U R V I A G J R Q Q L K B J W D M W G
T X A B L O U F C H A Y I K Y S U P A E
B P U D Q C A H M B C O V K W U X C Y J
Z I X I H D Y N K Z W V M N F D M O Q O
O X Q T E T P L G S O X C J B A W I Y C
G W Q B W V X I Z K I G X C I K V O Y O
H W U I U G Q G P K H H N U M Y X Z G I
U W S A W E K N K C P V L F B H I H S B
J U C G X J M W A Z I L W E N W B W I Y
C O E V W O W J T U A J O Z J F X O C J
X U Z K J K O Z O W D E H G S Q Z X V C
S M K N H H Q W X E M T C I Q A Q L O I
L J F D S D I R L P K Z C I Z P V Y M Z
U S I W V A V S Z C C V X D A K H L J Y
B M D X C T E U P V J M A P U X V I Z L
K E O A E U A I R T R O M K I X W V L H
J I W Z R D B E K P Q M G B L Z Y E Q G
```

TICK OFF THE WORDS AS YOU FIND THEM...

- [ ] **BO**
- [ ] **SO**
- [ ] **DO**
- [ ] **SHO**
- [ ] **FO**
- [ ] **KRO**
- [ ] **FRO**
- [ ] **PO**
- [ ] **NO**
- [ ] **RO**
- [ ] **TRO**
- [ ] **TO**
- [ ] **LO**
- [ ] **PLO**
- [ ] **BLO**

The Judoon are mercenary rhinos who think they're intergalactic police. If you're on their wanted list, they'll stop at nothing to arrest you. Warning — pulling off a Judoon's horn is considered a massive insult, so try not to do that.

ANSWERS ON PAGE 61

CONTINUED ON PAGE 37

CAPTAIN JACK'S DALEK FILES

PART 2

DALEK VS DALEK

From the moment they were created, the Daleks have been convinced of one thing: that they're the ultimate form of life. That means they've always been obsessed with weeding out any new mutations – all changes to the formula must be exterminated!

IMPERIAL DALEKS

After the Daleks exterminated Davros, they were forced to bring him back to life to help them fight yet another war. He was still sore about how he'd been treated, so he plotted to wipe out the original Daleks with a virus, then build a new, more loyal army – the Imperial Daleks!

RENEGADE DALEKS

Some of the original Daleks survived Davros' purge and became known as the Renegade Daleks. They wanted to wipe out the Imperial Daleks, because the Imperials weren't pure in their Dalekness. The Renegades and Imperials both turned up on Earth in 1963 and began blowing each other to bits on the streets of London.

TIME WAR DALEKS

The 'real' Daleks got a shiny golden glow-up to fight the Last Great Time War against the Time Lords. It was a brutal conflict, and every single Dalek was presumed destroyed – but one ship survived. The Emperor then broke every rule by making millions of new Daleks from harvested humans!

THE CULT OF SKARO

The Emperor's new army was obliterated, but four very special Daleks remained. The Cult of Skaro had been given the job of thinking the unthinkable to make sure the Daleks survived – including creating human-Dalek hybrids! Their leader, Dalek Sec, was exterminated by the others for – surprise! – not being Dalek-y enough.

THE NEW DALEK EMPIRE

Davros, presumed dead after the Time War, made a further comeback, and soon got busy building another new empire. To make sure the Daleks' DNA was pure, he made each one from a single cell of his own Kaled body. (Eew, gross.)

THE NEW DALEK PARADIGM

The last few Dalek drones left in the universe crash-landed on Earth, and this bunch of scavenging survivors had one last trick up their sleeves. They used a Progenitor – a device holding pure Dalek DNA – to create five shiny new Daleks. Bigger and more colourful than any Daleks ever seen before, they didn't think much of the 'unclean' drones who had brought them to life, so blasted them to atoms seconds later. Very harsh!

DEATH SQUAD DALEKS

When Jack Robertson and Leo Rugazzi accidentally created a new army of Daleks from the remains of a damaged Reconnaissance Dalek on Earth, the Doctor summoned a Dalek death squad. Their job was to hunt down mutant strains, so the Doctor knew they'd take out the new models. They did, blasting every single one to smithereens.

BAD BUSINESS

with JACK ROBERTSON

CEO, The Robertson Corporation

They say the first rule of business is that the customer is always right. Wrong! The *real* first rule of business is: do whatever you like, as long as you don't kill the customer. And if you do happen to kill the customer, is that really so bad? My spies tell me that some of the best businesses this side of Mars have been known to make the odd mistake . . .

BAD WOLF CORPORATION

THE BUSINESS PLAN: An alien race called the Daleks, who I have never seen or heard of before, set up a TV station broadcasting non-stop game shows. They beamed humans in and forced them to be contestants – before turning the losers into more of these Daleks. Everybody wins! Well, except the losers . . .

THE FATAL FLAW: The Doctor, Captain Jack and their friend Rose didn't want to play, so fought the Daleks to put an end to their gruesome games.

CYBUS INDUSTRIES

THE BUSINESS PLAN: Businessman John Lumic set up a telecoms business selling wireless headsets, but it was all a cover! His real goal was to gain control of the population and turn them into his personal army of Cybermen. Very enterprising!

THE FATAL FLAW: Lumic's creations turned him into a Cyberman as well, then the signal guiding everyone to the Cyber factories for conversion was blocked by the Doctor.

THE ROBERTSON CORPORATION

THE BUSINESS PLAN: The world's most gifted, handsome and modest businessman, Jack Robertson, bounced back from an unfortunate toxic-waste-and-mutant-spider scandal (that absolutely wasn't his fault) by going into partnership with the British technology minister, Jo Patterson.

With the world in turmoil and civil unrest growing, Jo knew the Robertson Corporation's stunning new Defence Drones were just what she needed to convince everyone she was the right person to lead her country. Especially when Jack secretly cut her in on a slice of the profits. (Shh, don't tell anyone that part!)

THE FATAL FLAW: This plan is absolutely flawless, and nothing can possibly go wrong. We are just about to enter final regional beta testing, and soon the world will witness the awesome power of the Defence Drones.

VOR

THE BUSINESS PLAN: Bitter business boss Daniel Barton made a deal with the alien Kasaavin to sell the human race for use as living data storage. He planned to use their own phones to wipe their minds.

THE FATAL FLAW: Aided by Ada Lovelace and Noor Inayat Khan, the Doctor seeded a failsafe system into every electronic device ever built, which sent the Kasaavin back to their own dimension. Typical brainboxes – never thinking of the bottom line.

KERBLAM!

THE BUSINESS PLAN: Kerblam! sent robot delivery men all over the universe, delivering parcels to happy customers.

THE FATAL FLAW: Every single parcel for delivery was packed with explosive bubble wrap by Charlie, a worker opposed to robots taking all the humans' jobs! Definitely something to bring up in his next performance review.

MONSTER CELLMATES
THE SYCORAX

JUDOON MAXIMUM SECURITY FACILITY
CRIMINAL RECORD

PRISONER
Clyde

ORIGIN
The Fire Trap, JX82

CRIMES
Blood control, enslaving humanity

SENTENCE
Solitary confinement

DANGER RATING

1 2 3 4 5

ANGRY RED EYES

CEREMONIAL BONE HELMET

SKINLESS FACE WITH SHARP TEETH UNDER EXOSKELETON

TRADITIONAL WARRIOR ROBES

>>> The Sycorax like to give the impression they're technologically advanced, but most of their gear is stolen.

>>> The majority of their skills are also plundered from other races. One favourite is the ability to take control of everyone with a particular blood type.

>>> They often use blackmail to get what they want.

>>> The Sycorax claim to be honourable warriors, but their reliance on violence, intimidation and slavery reveals their true nature.

>>> They have excellent armed-combat skills. You would have to be very brave to take one on in a sword fight.

KNOWN SIGHTINGS:

102
The Pandorica, Stonehenge, Earth

2006
Spaceship in orbit above Earth

UNKNOWN FUTURE DATE
Zaggit Zagoo

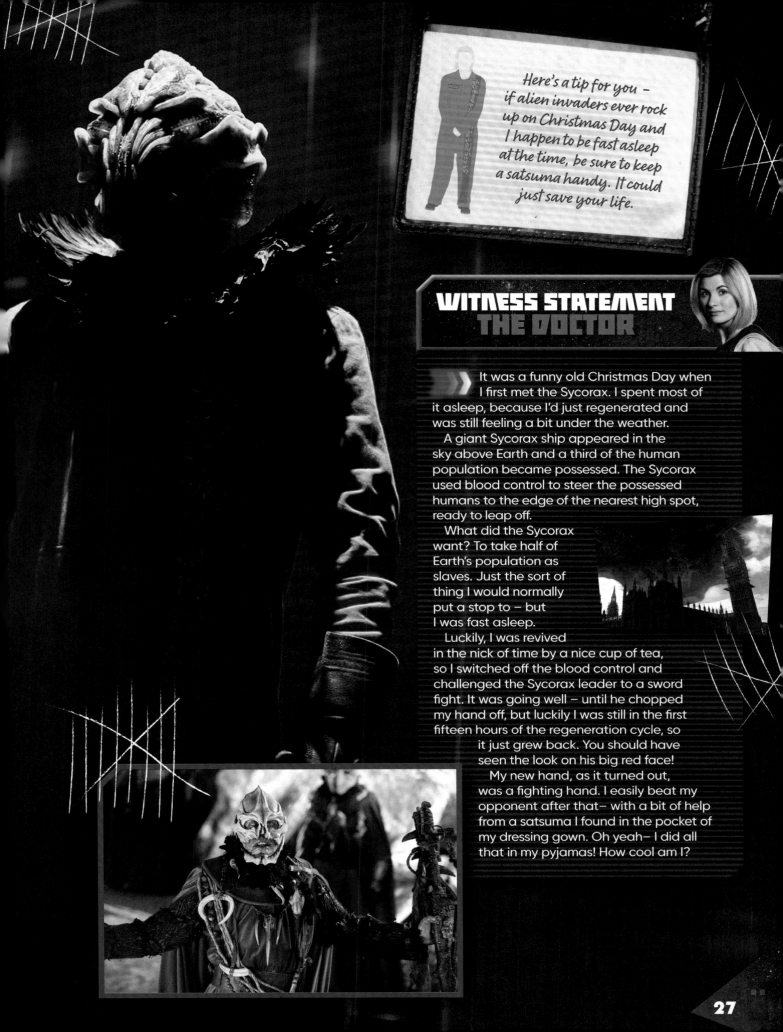

Here's a tip for you – if alien invaders ever rock up on Christmas Day and I happen to be fast asleep at the time, be sure to keep a satsuma handy. It could just save your life.

WITNESS STATEMENT
THE DOCTOR

It was a funny old Christmas Day when I first met the Sycorax. I spent most of it asleep, because I'd just regenerated and was still feeling a bit under the weather.

A giant Sycorax ship appeared in the sky above Earth and a third of the human population became possessed. The Sycorax used blood control to steer the possessed humans to the edge of the nearest high spot, ready to leap off.

What did the Sycorax want? To take half of Earth's population as slaves. Just the sort of thing I would normally put a stop to – but I was fast asleep.

Luckily, I was revived in the nick of time by a nice cup of tea, so I switched off the blood control and challenged the Sycorax leader to a sword fight. It was going well – until he chopped my hand off, but luckily I was still in the first fifteen hours of the regeneration cycle, so it just grew back. You should have seen the look on his big red face!

My new hand, as it turned out, was a fighting hand. I easily beat my opponent after that– with a bit of help from a satsuma I found in the pocket of my dressing gown. Oh yeah– I did all that in my pyjamas! How cool am I?

TOP

You might think your street is just a run-of-the-mill kind of street, but have you ever thought there could be an alien base below it? Or a Dalek factory, hidden inside the post box? OK, maybe not the post box – perhaps your next-door-neighbour's garden shed. Here are some other Earth locations hiding incredible secrets . . .

CANARY WHARF, LONDON

One Canada Square is usually home to thousands of office workers, but it also used to be home to the Torchwood Institute: a secret organisation dedicated to protecting Britain from alien threats. It didn't stay secret for long – not after two mighty armies of Daleks and Cybermen had a massive battle in its HQ. What do you mean, you don't remember that? Honestly! Humans.

CARDIFF, WALES

The capital city of Wales is brilliant in many ways, but one of them isn't something everyone knows. Cardiff sits on a space-time rift and is absolutely crackling with power, making it a magnet for alien invasions and strange anomalies. Captain Jack used to run a branch of Torchwood there – it was right below the Water Tower on Roald Dahl Plass. After my hand got chopped off by the Sycorax, it spent a while in the Torchwood Hub, bubbling away in a jar.

MADAGASCAR

I spent some time on a lovely beach on this beautiful island – but there was no chance of getting in a spot of sunbathing. I was investigating deadly bacteria, plus some weird bird behaviour. An alien infection had been attracted to Earth by all the plastic here – dinner time!

SECRET!

NOVOSIBIRSK, SIBERIA

If you win a free holiday to a paradise spa, always check whether it's actually paradise first. Me and the fam left on this particular trip in a bit of a hurry, so it was a surprise to discover that Tranquillity Spa on the planet Orphan 55 was actually built near the ruins of Novosibirsk. In this timeline, Earth, ravaged by nuclear war and climate change, had been renamed to warn-off potential visitors.

OSAKA, JAPAN

This might look like an ordinary building in an ordinary agricultural park, but inside it's a Dalek clone farm! Hundreds of tanks rise up as far as the eye can see, each one containing a freshly grown, wriggling, squelching Dalek mutant. Don't try sneaking in, because those mutants love to stretch their tentacles to deal with unwanted visitors!

GREAT VICTORIA DESERT, AUSTRALIA

Every TARDIS has a clever thing called a Chameleon Circuit, which is meant to allow it to change form and blend in wherever it lands. I've never been one for blending in, but the Master really pulled the wool over my eyes by disguising his as a wooden house in the Australian outback. So sneaky! It didn't look quite so inconspicuous when we saw it flying, mind you.

WHAT'S THE TIME FOR YOU?
PAST, PRESENT OR FUTURE?

Let the TARDIS detect your personal time-travelling style! First, tick your five fave scenes from some of the Doctor's adventures . . .

Nikola Tesla's Night of Terror

Resolution

Praxeus

Demons of the Punjab

The Tsuranga Conundrum

Ascension of the Cybermen

Kerblam!

The Witchfinders

Fugitive of the Judoon

Orphan 55

Rosa

The Battle of Ranskoor Av Kolos

Arachnids in the UK

Spyfall

It Takes You Away

Next, count up how many boxes you've ticked of each colour. The TARDIS navigation systems will analyse your choices and whisk you off to the destination of your dreams . . .

MOSTLY RED
THE PAST *Like Graham*

Spot on, kiddo – you're just like me. I'm sure travelling a gazillion years into the future is all well and good, but there are too many killer robots, mutated humans and extinction events for my liking. No, give me a nice trip into the past any day! You can't beat meeting some of the most amazing people from Earth's history: Rosa Parks, King James I, Mary Shelley, Lord Byron – you name 'em, I've had a good natter with 'em!

MOSTLY SILVER
THE PRESENT *Like Ryan*

I've been hundreds of years into the past, then right to the end of time – but I reckon living in the here and now is the best. There's so much going on, and I don't want to miss a second of it! How could I ever be bored, with environmental danger, space rhinos, Dalek battle fleets and scary dudes who are more teeth than face right here on my doorstep? Plus, I've just ordered that new PS5 . . .

MOSTLY BLUE
THE FUTURE *Like Yaz*

I'm happy to go wherever the TARDIS takes me for as long as it wants to take me there, but there's something really incredible about seeing what the future has in store. After all, living in the present can be scary, so it's good to see how everything turns out. I figure that, if I know what's coming, then there's a chance I can help make the future a better place.

CAPTAIN JACK'S DALEK FILES

PART 3

SQUIDS IN!

By now you know all about the outside of a Dalek, but what's lurking inside that tough Dalekanium shell? Hope you're not squeamish, because it ain't pretty!

INSIDE THE DALEK

Every Dalek has two parts: the mechanical life-supporting armour and the genetically engineered, multi-tentacled organic mutant. Or, to put it another way, the shell and the squid.

Occasionally Dalek shells are mobile without a mutant inside, or the creature waves a tentacle at the outside world, but they usually come as a pair.

The mutant is generally made up of a large brain sitting on top of a mass of tentacles, with at least one eye. It sits in the Dalek Heart – a central chamber filled with all the proteins necessary to stay alive.

In some early Dalek models the tentacles directly operated the machine's systems. They later evolved the ability to control their systems using a positronic link.

INSIDE THE DALEK

Sometimes a Dalek mutant can become separated from its shell. When that happens, the creature goes into survival mode. It will launch itself at the face of any creature that poses a threat – something I found out the hard way, when one gave me a big Dalek kiss!

Its next priority is to get itself a new host body. If it captures a human, it will attach itself to the victim's back, then make a direct connection to their brain by plunging a tentacle into their neck. Once the mutant has control of the human's brain and movements, the poor victim is totally under the mutant's control – still conscious, but nothing more than a puppet.

THE FIRST DALEK ON EARTH

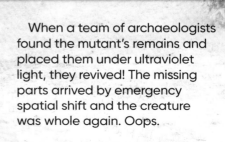

When the first Reconnaissance Dalek arrived on Earth from Skaro, armies from all over the world came together to battle it. They managed to win – just!

The humans destroyed the Dalek's shell and carved the mutant into three parts, which they buried at secret locations around the world.

But one mutant section never reached its intended destination. It spent the next few centuries somewhere under Sheffield Town Hall.

When a team of archaeologists found the mutant's remains and placed them under ultraviolet light, they revived! The missing parts arrived by emergency spatial shift and the creature was whole again. Oops.

INSIDE NUMBER 10

with Yaz

The prime minister's job is to lead the government, making sure the country's safe and everyone's looked after. The Doctor's met several occupants of 10 Downing Street. For most, it was a great honour to live behind that famous black door – but others had their own agendas . . .

WINSTON CHURCHILL

The Doctor's such a namedropper! I haven't heard of half the people she claims to be mates with, but I definitely knew about this guy. You've probably heard of him too – Churchill led his country in World War II and helped defeat the Nazis. But you might not know about the Doctor dropping in on him in 1941 – a scientist had invented these machines called Ironsides, and old Winnie thought they'd help him win the war. But they were camouflaged Daleks! The scientist was a robot the Daleks had built and programmed to think it had invented them. Sneaky!

JOSEPH GREEN

You won't remember all this – the Doctor rebooted the universe or something – but the prime minister was killed in 2006 by a rogue gang of trumping aliens called the Slitheen. One of them, Jocrassa Fel-Fotch Passameer-Day Slitheen, nabbed the vacant job for himself by squeezing his massive booty into the skin of Joseph Green, an MP he had killed. The Slitheen then launched a missile at 10 Downing Street, but got blown to little green bits when they didn't escape in time.

HARRIET JONES

This incredible woman was once just the humble MP for Flydale North, but, after proving herself during the Doctor's battle against the Slitheen, she took over as prime minister. She and the Doctor didn't always see eye to eye – her time at the top came to a swift end when she shot down a retreating alien ship. Later, she risked her life by running a secret comms channel to bring the Doctor's friends together to defeat the Daleks. Sadly, the Daleks tracked her signal, and she died a hero, defending the Earth.

HAROLD SAXON

Mr Saxon seemed to appear from nowhere, then boom! He was prime minister. Saxon showed his true colours when he summoned the Toclafane – alien spheres armed with very sharp blades – to slice and dice a tenth of the Earth's population. He wasn't really a politician at all – he was the Master. And the Toclafane weren't aliens; they were future humans, brought back to kill their own ancestors. The Doctor managed to sort things out by rewinding time, so you might not remember very much about Mr Saxon either . . .

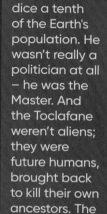

JO PATTERSON

This is our latest PM. Or she will be, soon, if the opinion polls are anything to go by. There's something about her that I really don't like, though. She's obsessed with security, and mad about law and order. There are rumours online that she's planning some kind of new Defence Drone, and that she's friendly with Spiders Guy – Jack Robertson. I wish the Doctor was here, so we could find out exactly what she's up to . . .

MONSTROUS MASH-UP

Look closely –
can you match
the beastly bits in this
mash-up creature to
their owners? All except
one of the monsters
below appear, and one
is already matched
to start you off!

■1

■2

■3

■4

■5

■6

■7

■8

■9

■10

■11

■12

7

ANSWERS ON PAGE 61

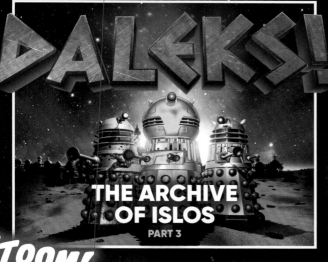

CONTINUED ON PAGE 47

MONSTER CELLMATES
THE PTING

JUDOON MAXIMUM SECURITY FACILITY
CRIMINAL RECORD

-)) **PRISONER**
  Tiny

-)) **ORIGIN**
  Unknown

-)) **CRIMES**
  Greed, extreme violence

-)) **SENTENCE**
  Containment in electric cage

-)) **DANGER RATING**

1 2 3 4 5

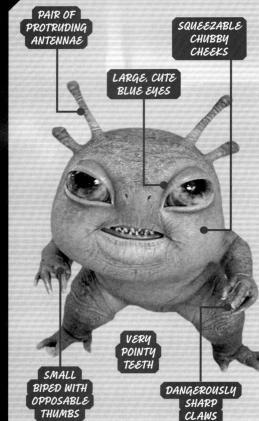

PAIR OF PROTRUDING ANTENNAE

LARGE, CUTE BLUE EYES

SQUEEZABLE CHUBBY CHEEKS

SMALL BIPED WITH OPPOSABLE THUMBS

VERY POINTY TEETH

DANGEROUSLY SHARP CLAWS

)) Pting might look adorable, but they're actually dangerously destructive.

)) A Pting is capable of scoffing any kind of non-organic material.

)) Pting skin is incredibly toxic – look, but definitely don't touch!

)) Pting have evolved to survive in extreme temperatures.

)) Pting aren't malicious, but they are naturally driven to acts of terrible violence and destruction.

)) Pting can survive in the vacuum of space.

)) Pting are absolutely impossible to kill!

KNOWN SIGHTINGS:

SIXTY-SEVENTH CENTURY
The *Tsuranga*, deep space

UNKNOWN
Judoon prison

Sometimes, the smallest creature can pose the biggest threat. Take my little mate Tiny here. Looks like butter wouldn't melt in his mouth, doesn't he? But that mouth is one of the most dangerous mouths you ever to encounter . . .

WITNESS STATEMENT
THE DOCTOR

I was on board a medical ship in the far future, with no TARDIS and no obvious means of escape – never a good position to be in when there's a Pting on the loose!

The Pting is small, but its appetite is mighty. It will eat literally anything its sharp little gnashers come into contact with. Well, apart from anything that's actually alive – luckily for us, it won't touch meat. But spaceships? One Pting can devour a whole one, then scoff the escape pod for afters.

Me and the fam thought we'd end up floating among the stars. This greedy little blighter was intent on eating the floors right out from under us! I tricked the Pting into snacking on the ship's antimatter core, which he thought was delicious – until it blew up.

It's impossible to actually kill a Pting, so it's still floating around out there somewhere. Hope it doesn't like big, blue boxes or I could end up in mighty trouble.

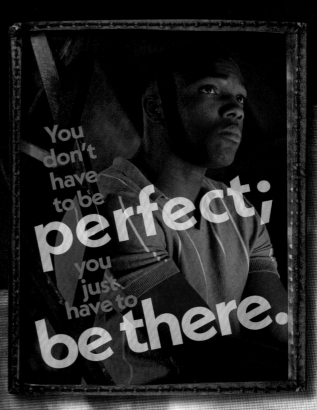

You don't have to be perfect; you just have to be there.

PSYCHIC

Everyone loves a new wallpaper for their phone or computer, and I'm just the same – except mine appear on my psychic paper, when it's not busy being psychic! Here are a few of my faves . . .

Lives change worlds. People can save planets or wreck them.

THAT'S THE CHOICE.

Let me take it from the top. Hello, I'm the Doctor. I'm a traveller in space and time, and that thing buried down there is called a TARDIS.

YOU'RE GONNA LOVE THIS.

I'M THE DOCTOR

THE ONE WHO STOPS THE DALEKS

Wall PAPER

Go on, son . . .

YOU'RE DOING IT, MATE!

WHERE

TO

NEXT?

I was thinking . . . everywhere!

Hey there. My name is Leo Rugazzi and I'm the CEO of Rugazzi Technologies.

My company has been developing some super-cool new tech that's so top secret, I'm not sure I'm even allowed to tell myself about it. We're thinking big – cloning!

I've been working with Jack Robertson, who has provided me with reference material about other cloning and duplication operations. I don't know where he gets this stuff from – some of it even seems to come from the future. But it's all going to help me make something totally revolutionary. I can't wait to show it to you . . .

CREEPY CLONES
AND DEADLY DUPLICATES

GANGERS

Right now, on Earth, there's a company called Morpeth Jetsan, and there are all kinds of rumours about what they're up to. Some say they're trying to create the first human doppelgangers – Gangers, for short. These Gangers could do all the dangerous work, while the owner of the original mind was safe at home watching cartoons. There would be some boring ethical questions about their rights as living beings, but we can gloss over that.

AUTONS

You'd be amazed how many aliens seem to want to come to Earth just to open up a factory. Surely they could think of something more fun to do? The Nestene Consciousness was no different when it rocked up here. It set up an operation called Auto Plastics, whose purpose was to create Autons – plastic robots who looked like everyday things. Dummies, dolls, waxworks – if it's plastic, it could be an Auton. There's even a rumour that some Autons are still here on Earth, left behind after the failed invasion. I need to get over to Madame Tussauds soon to investigate . . .

SONTARANS

Around 2008, there was an attempt by aliens to invade Earth. I know! An alien attack that was completely covered up by the establishment! Can you believe it?

The would-be invaders were Sontarans – a race of cloned warriors who needed a new planet on which to grow more soldiers. They didn't look very impressive – think Humpty Dumpty but without the wall – and all they ever wanted to do was fight. I guess that's why they went through so many clones.

A bratty genius called Luke Rattigan was helping them. He invented the ATMOS system for cars, which was designed to release poison gas that would wipe out all life, leaving the Earth clear for a Sontaran clone farm.

In the end, Luke realised the Sontarans had tricked him and sacrificed himself to save the planet. What a loser. I would never be so dumb!

CAPTAIN JACK'S  FILES

EXTERMINATE!

Every Dalek is armed and extremely dangerous – a single unit could wipe out the entire population of a planet! Here are the lethal weapons you need to know about if you want to survive . . .

THE GUN

A Dalek's gun stick is its main (and most deadly) weapon. It shoots a ferocious bolt of inverted photon energy that surrounds the victim. Anyone hit by a Dalek's shot will look like a living X-ray – you will see their skeleton and internal organs.

One blast is enough to kill most people. It's like being hit by lightning! The energy ray scrambles the victim's insides, and can reduce them to dust. Time Lords are sometimes able to regenerate if they haven't taken the full force of the hit.

The gun can also take out entire buildings, so don't try to escape by running indoors. A Dalek could blast your house to smithereens in seconds!

WATCH OUT FOR pools of water or sprinklers – a Dalek energy blast will travel through water and fry anything organic it makes contact with!

⊙ THE MANIPULATOR

The gun isn't the only dangerous part of a Dalek. Its other accessory might look just like a sink plunger to you, but it can do some serious damage!

A Dalek's right arm is usually telescopic, with a tool on the end. The standard 'sucker' arm is used for connecting to the systems on a Dalek battleship, or to operate other machinery.

Some Daleks have a heat-cutting arm instead of the plunger – handy for burning through solid doors. Others have an actual flamethrower.

Some more appendages you might spot are grabber claws, syringes, receiver dishes and, just once, a little tray serving up afternoon tea.

WATCH OUT FOR the sucker arm coming near your face – the Daleks can use it to extract knowledge from your brain or suffocate you to death!

DEFENCE DRONES

When Leo Rugazzi was building Jack Robertson's Defence Drones, he didn't know they were really Daleks – but he still equipped them with some serious weapons . . .

Leo says:

The unit's built-in water cannon is handy for dispersing unruly crowds.

Protesters not afraid of a soaking? Turn the CS gas on them instead! That'll bring tears to their eyes.

If all else fails, a quick blast of the on-board sonic deterrent system will really get their ears ringing.

DALEK DESIGN CHALLENGE

DALEK UNIT HAS LOST WEAPONS AND TOOLS. REPLACEMENTS MUST BE DESIGNED. YOU, SMALL HUMAN, WILL USE THE KNOWLEDGE SHARED BY CAPTAIN JACK HARKNESS TO DESIGN A REPLACEMENT SYSTEM! **OBEY! OBEY! OBEY!**

DRAW YOUR WEAPON OR TOOL HERE

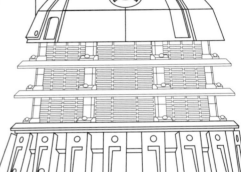

ASSIGN YOUR DRONE A COLOUR

THIS IS A

ITS PURPOSE IS

YOU HAVE DONE WELL. NOW YOU WILL BE EXTERMINATED. EXTERMINATE! EXTERMINATE! *EXTERMINAAAAAATE!*

DALEKS!

THE ARCHIVE OF ISLOS
PART 4

The portal crackles and fizzes to reveal a strange, wild vortex...

FZZZ!

TELL THE EMPEROR. TELL HIM WHAT YOU HAVE DONE.

THE POPULATION HAS GONE *THROUGH THE PORTAL*, ALONG WITH THE CONTENTS OF THE ARCHIVE.

"THE DALEKS HAVE CAPTURED AN EMPTY BUILDING."

IMPOSSIBLE!

YOU HAVE BETRAYED THE DALEKS. YOU WILL BE EXTERMINATED.

ZZZZT!

YOU WILL ALL BE EXTERMINATED.

ARRGGGH!

BZZZT!

WAIT. CONFESS!

THE CHIEF ARCHIVIAN COMES FORWARD . . .

I DID IT. I FOUND DETAILS OF A RACE IN THE ARCHIVE. A RACE *ANCIENT* AND *OUTSIDE OF TIME.*

THE PORTAL ACTIVATES, AND A VAST GREEN CLOUD OF ENERGY APPROACHES!

FZZZ!

THEY OPENED THE PORTAL AND OFFERED US *SANCTUARY.*

THIS RACE – ALL LIFE WANTS SOMETHING. WHAT DID YOU OFFER THEM IN RETURN FOR RESCUE?

WHAT DID YOU OFFER THEM?

WE OFFERED THEM . . .

YOU

TO BE CONTINUED!
SEE HOW THE STORY ENDS BY WATCHING ALL OF *DALEKS!* ON THE OFFICIAL DOCTOR WHO YOUTUBE CHANNEL.

THE DIVISION

So, quick recap. Turns out I wasn't born on Gallifrey, and I've lived a much longer life than I ever imagined. So why can't I remember any of it? And what was I actually doing all that time?

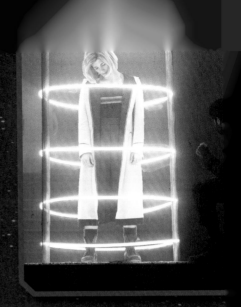

The Matrix is where all Time Lord knowledge is stored, but nobody ever knew the truth about the Timeless Child because it was hidden by Tecteun! Then the Master showed me everything.

The tale of Tecteun and the child was disguised as the story of Brendan, a baby taken in by the couple who found him abandoned in Ireland.

When Brendan was all grown up, he joined the Gardaí, the Irish police.

He had an accident where he fell backwards off a cliff, exactly as the Timeless Child did. And, like her, Brendan didn't die – he just got back up and carried on with his life.

He stayed in the Gardaí until retirement, when he was presented with a special clock by his boss. Brendan was old but the sergeant had never aged. The sergeant thanked Brendan for his service but said he'd have to wipe his memory. Huh?

As the Master played me the false memory of Brendan's mind being wiped, I noticed the inscription on the back of Brendan's new clock. A dedication for services to the Division.

The Timeless Child also worked for the Division; a secret Time Lord agency that was allowed to break the rules about interfering in other worlds and times. This is where it gets complicated . . .

The next part of this story had already happened to me – in Gloucester, when a platoon of Judoon arrived looking for a fugitive. This person on the run was none other than the Timeless Child – me.

The Doctor had obviously decided life in the Division wasn't for her, so headed to Earth, where she disguised herself as a human named Ruth. The Division didn't like that one bit, and a Gallifreyan called Gat sent the Judoon to bring her back 'for the glory of Gallifrey'.

What happened next? And how does it all fit in to my life now? Those are answers I still don't have – but I promised Ryan that I'd find them, so I'd better get cracking. Watch this space . . .

MONSTER CELLMATES
THE SILENCE

))) **PRISONER**
What prisoner?

))) **ORIGIN**
The Church of the Papal Mainframe

))) **CRIMES**
Stealth invasion

))) **SENTENCE**
Constant surveillance

))) **DANGER RATING**

1 2 3 4 5

HUMANOID WITH BULBOUS HEAD

HANDS WITH THREE EXTRA-LONG FINGERS AND A SHORT THUMB

TINY EYES SET BACK IN SKULL

USUALLY DRESSED IN A BLACK SUIT

CAN SHOOT BLASTS OF DEADLY ENERGY FROM FINGERS

))) Anyone who sees the Silence immediately forgets when they look elsewhere.

))) Victims can have flashbacks if they see a Silent again, but these aren't permanent.

))) Can plant hypnotic suggestions in the mind of anyone who sees them.

))) To attack, the Silence draw electrical energy out of the atmosphere around them, then shoot it out their long fingers.

KNOWN SIGHTINGS:

1969

2011

THE FALL OF THE ELEVENTH

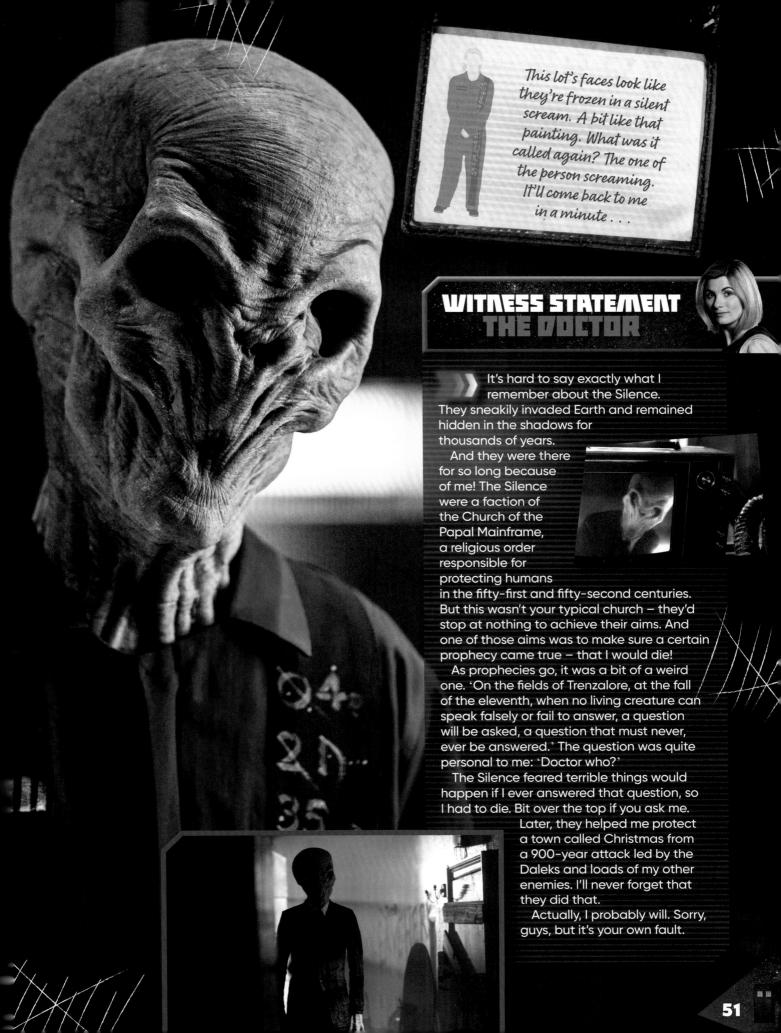

This lot's faces look like they're frozen in a silent scream. A bit like that painting. What was it called again? The one of the person screaming. It'll come back to me in a minute . . .

WITNESS STATEMENT
THE DOCTOR

It's hard to say exactly what I remember about the Silence. They sneakily invaded Earth and remained hidden in the shadows for thousands of years.

And they were there for so long because of me! The Silence were a faction of the Church of the Papal Mainframe, a religious order responsible for protecting humans in the fifty-first and fifty-second centuries. But this wasn't your typical church – they'd stop at nothing to achieve their aims. And one of those aims was to make sure a certain prophecy came true – that I would die!

As prophecies go, it was a bit of a weird one. 'On the fields of Trenzalore, at the fall of the eleventh, when no living creature can speak falsely or fail to answer, a question will be asked, a question that must never, ever be answered.' The question was quite personal to me: 'Doctor who?'

The Silence feared terrible things would happen if I ever answered that question, so I had to die. Bit over the top if you ask me.

Later, they helped me protect a town called Christmas from a 900-year attack led by the Daleks and loads of my other enemies. I'll never forget that they did that.

Actually, I probably will. Sorry, guys, but it's your own fault.

SCARY CHRISTMAS
AND UNHAPPY NEW YEAR

1

Who can forget the time I had to deal with a spinning Christmas tree of death?

2

Oh, and did you know what looks like Santa is sometimes actually a killer robot?

3

One year, I celebrated on the space liner *Titanic*. Guess what? It didn't sink! But it did nearly crash into Buckingham Palace.

4

The next Christmas was ruined by having to fight off Cybermen in the snow – and they'd brought along their nasty little pets, the Cybershades!

5

I spent one Christmas and New Year battling to avert the end of time. And then I regenerated! Busy year.

6

First Christmas in a new body. No chance for a rest – not while there were flying sharks to deal with!

7

This was a truly magical festive season – there was even a Wooden King!

The festive season is traditionally a time to relax, when the most dangerous thing you're likely to do is open too many selection boxes. My Christmas and New Year celebrations tend to be more eventful . . .

8

Three words: Snowmen. Are. Alive.

9

Only I could have a Christmas that lasted more than 900 years, all spent defending a town called Christmas against almost every monster in the universe.

10

OK, I have to admit, this was a good one – I got to spend it with the real Father Christmas! And some monsters, but you can't have everything.

11

This one was confusing. People kept getting their heads chopped off.

12

One Christmas I hung out with an actual superhero! How cool is that?

13

Heard the story about the two armies that met in no man's land on Christmas Day for a game of footy? I was there!

14

Not so keen on Christmas in this current body; I prefer New Year for some reason. Well, can you blame me, after the Christmases I've had? My resolution is the same every year – to defeat the Daleks!

CAPTAIN JACK'S DALEK FILES

PART 5

MADE IN BRITAIN

RECONNAISSANCE DALEK

The Reconnaissance Dalek was one of the first Daleks to leave Skaro in search of planets and people to conquer.

It arrived on Earth but faced fierce resistance. Its casing was destroyed, and the mutant inside carved up and buried.

Eventually, the mutant was restored to life. Its priority was to build a new casing.

The mutant took control of a human host and visited a weapons company that bought alien artefacts on the black market. It found its original gun and parts of its shell.

The mutant forced its human puppet to build a new shell using leftover pieces of the original casing, plus modern scrap metal. It was vulnerable to microwaves, and a handy oven melted it.

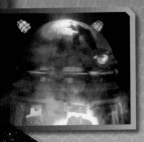

The damaged unit was retrieved and sent to storage – but was intercepted and ended up in the hands of Leo Rugazzi, boss of a technology company.

These two Daleks were unlike those that came before. Meet the Reconnaissance Dalek and the Defence Drone . . .

DEFENCE DRONE

⬡ Leo studied the Dalek's shell to find out exactly how it worked. He used this research to build a copy.

⬡ His new model was entirely robotic, with no creature inside – just advanced tech. Its artificial-intelligence interface was programmed for every eventuality.

⬡ The unit was heavily armoured with weapons and rocket boosters. It was designed to be used for prison security, events and border control.

⬡ Thousands of Defence Drones were 3D-printed in refurbished car plants in the UK.

⬡ But these were no passive drones. Leo had found traces of the original Dalek mutant, and cloned these cells to grow a new one! The mutant started its own cloning plant, and adapted Leo's design to accommodate the freshly - grown mutants.

⬡ The new Dalek units glowed bright blue – until the cloned mutants took up residence, when they changed to a fierce red.

BREAKING

I've been locked up for a very long time, but I've never had any doubt that I'd get out – not really. Me and my mates have been in a few tight spots in our time but we always managed to escape. In fact, I'm sure I just heard someone knocking . . .

INCOGNITO EXIT

There are definitely better places to be trapped than a spaceship packed with sleeping Cybermen, but luckily Yaz and Graham are a very resourceful duo. Just as the Cyber army came to life, they nicked a couple of cyber suits then stomped out of the Cybercarrier.

SKY HIGH!

Graham, Ryan and Yaz were left high and dry when the Master trapped them on a plane with no cockpit! I'd been sent off to a mysterious alien realm with no way of getting back, so there was nothing I could do. Or was there? I went back in time to plant some special safety instructions under a seat. Using these, the fam were able to land the plane safely. Result!

FREE!

Ok, this is a new one. I'm writing this on to my psychic paper as the escape is actually happening! It all started when I heard that knocking. Was someone trying to get my attention from the next cell? I found out at exercise time, when I came face-to-face with my old friend Captain Jack Harkness. He's just pulled a little gadget out of his pocket.

Says it's a gateway disinhibitor – not a very catchy name, is it? Oh, he calls it a Breakout Ball – of course he does. He's pressing it, and now we're in a bubble. Can't remember the last time I was in a bubble. We're moving now, but Jack says the bubble isn't going to last long, so we run and run. Just eleven seconds until the bubble bursts and . . .

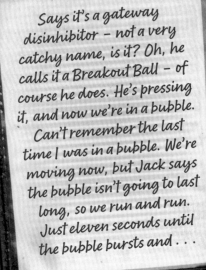

WITCH WAY OUT?

A trip to seventeenth-century Lancashire saw me accused of being a witch, then tied to a chair, ready to be bobbed underwater. If I came back up alive, I was definitely a witch and would be immediately sentenced to death. If I drowned, then I was definitely not a witch, and everyone would be extremely apologetic. Great. As luck would have it, I'm mates with Harry Houdini, one of the greatest escapologists who ever lived, so I was able to slip out of my bonds and swim to safety. Phew!

We've made it! We're in Jack's cell, and would you look at that, he's got a vortex manipulator hidden under the bed so we're really, really, really getting out of here. Incredible! Did you get all that? Make sure you remember it all, just in case the Judoon arrest you one day!

FAM FAREWELL

POLICE

GRAHAM'S TO-DO LIST

Start teaching the lad how to ride a bike. ✓

Help the Doc build a teleporter. ✓

Ask to go back in time to see Elvis play. ✓

Go back in time but don't end up seeing Elvis play. ✓

Professional networking with the bus drivers of Montgomery, Alabama. ✓

Kick-start a very important boycott. ✓

Pass on a letter to Ryan from his dad. ✓

Accidentally set off a sonic mine and knock everyone out. ✓

Witness a very special wedding on the day of the Partition of India. ✓

Get a little part-time job in the Kerblam! warehouse. Quit. ✓

Hang out with the Pendle Witches. ✓

Have one last conversation with my wife, Grace. ✓

Hear Ryan call me 'Grandad' for the very first time. ✓

Be the bigger man when facing down a murderous alien. ✓

Help Ryan get to know his dad better, in between fighting a rogue Dalek. ✓

Go a bit James Bond for an extremely dangerous mission. ✓

Briefly own a pair of laser shoes. ✓

Meet Thomas Edison and Nikola Tesla. ✓

Get a big smooch off a very friendly fella the Doctor used to know. ✓

Dress up as a Cyberman. ✓

Stop a revolution in its tracks. ✓

Decide it's time to retire from time-travelling. ✓

Finally get the lad going on that bike of his! ✓

BOX

TO-DO LIST – RYAN SINCLAIR

Fall off stupid bike.
Discover weird glowing alien pod.
Get electrocuted by electric coil creature.
Float around in actual space.
Race across desert planet.
Meet Rosa Parks and stand up for myself against racists.
Overcome my fear of spiders.
Overcome my fear of even bigger spiders.
Deliver baby of pregnant man.
Escape from 200 cyborg clones of Harry Houdini.
Visit the Punjab in 1947.
Ride the conveyer belt in the Kerblam! warehouse.
Get along really, really well with King James I.
See some weird stuff in Norway.
Fight in the Battle of Ranskoor Av Kolos.
Celebrate New Year nineteen times in a row, at different points in history.
Sort things out with my dad.
Wear a really cool tux!
Stop a Kasaavin invasion.
Go on a free holiday to a luxury spa.
Regret going on a free holiday to a luxury spa.
Investigate a mystery with a cool vlogger.
Drop in on my mate Tibo.
Realise I've been away from home too long.
Meet actual Mary Shelley (not Frankenstein though – or his monster).
Travel further forward in time than ever before.
Slam dunk some Cybermen.
Spend ten months back at home.
Think about how much my own planet needs me.
Have one last crazy adventure then say goodbye to the Doctor and Yaz.
Finally learn to ride that bike. (Well, nearly!)

Time travel? Completed it, mate!

My life has had lots of chapters, and it's always sad when one ends. Yaz and I will miss Graham and Ryan loads – but something tells me the TARDIS won't be quiet for long. Who knows – maybe you'll join me. What do YOU think might happen if you did?

WHAT THE FUTURE HOLDS

One day I was . . .

....

....

....

when a massive MONSTER suddenly appeared in front of me! It had . . .

○ **HEADS**   ○ **LEGS**   ○ **EYES**

○ **NOSES**   ○ **ARMS**   ○ **TENTACLES**

It was called

....

....

And it looked a bit like this:

This is Dan and he'll be joining the Doctor and Yaz in the TARDIS. What kind of adventures do you think they'll have together?

P8 FIENDISH FOURS

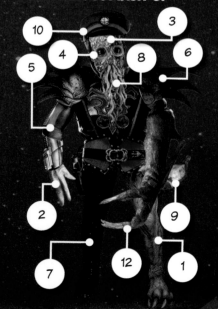

P20 BEAT THE JUDOON

```
D J P J L G W U Z H E R Y V D H V T H Q
H X P K X S R H D N C O U D U F V Z A U
D H I U I X N N P I I W Y M S I C Q Y C
P F I R K I H P F Q D V Z Y L Z A D K V
U Z N T X F S G N M N X A X S B I Y X Z
O W P V Q N Z Z C Q U O Z X S J F N C U
I C M P M G L Q P Z C V Q I C G T L G L
J U H D S P Y V E D H Z N N M P W C W N
H T E B F P B L W D E R D I T I O Y V G
E K U N Q C X W I X X S G B K M U V I M
Q W C R K R O X M O I Z I F D B S F O C
U U R V I A G J R Q Q L K B J W D M W G
T X A B L O U F C H A Y I K Y S U P A E
B P U D Q C A H M B C O V K W U X C Y J
Z I X I H D Y N K Z W V M N F D M O Q O
O X Q T E T P L G S O X C J B A W I Y C
G W Q B W V X I Z K I G X C I K V O Y O
H W U I U G Q G P K H H N U M Y X Z G I
U W S A W E K N K C P V L F B H I H S B
J U C G X J M W A Z I L W E N W B W I Y
C O E V W O W J T U A J O Z J F X O C J
X U Z K J K O Z O W D E H G S Q Z X V C
S M K N H H Q W X E M T C I Q A Q L O I
L J F D S D I R L P K Z C I Z P V Y M Z
U S I W V A V S Z C C V X D A K H L J Y
B M D X C T E U P V J M A P U X V I Z L
K E O A E U A I R T R O M K I X W V L H
J I W Z R D B E K P Q M G B L Z Y E Q G
```

P36 MONSTROUS MASH-UP

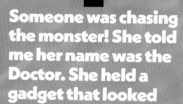

Someone was chasing the monster! She told me her name was the Doctor. She held a gadget that looked like this.

It looked a bit weird, but she was sure it would work. And it did! The monster . . .

 **EXPLODED.**

 **MELTED.**

VANISHED.

TURNED TO GUNGE.

The Doctor said I'd done brilliantly. She asked if I wanted to join her and I said:

YES **YES**

YES!